WALTER the WOLF

WALTER

Holiday House, New York

LIBRARY OF CONGRESS CATALOGING IN PUBLICATION DATA

Sharmat, Marjorie Weinman. Walter the Wolf.

SUMMARY: Tired of being perfect and never using his perfectly matched fangs, Walter the wolf yields to temptation. [1. Animals—Fiction. 2. Wolves—Fiction] I. Oechsli, Kelly, illus. II. Title. PZ7.S5299Wal [E] 74-26659 ISBN 0-8234-0253-3

the WOLF

By MARJORIE WEINMAN SHARMAT

with Pictures by
Kelly Oechsli

Once there was a wolf named Walter. He had horn-rimmed spectacles and two huge, perfectly matched fangs.

And there was something else about Walter.

He was perfect.

Being perfect was hard work. Walter did everything his mother told him to do. He practiced his violin two hours a day; he took singing lessons, and he wrote poetry. And he never used his fangs on other animals or people.

"Walter has the most unused fangs in the forest," everybody said. "And the biggest. Walter really should do something with his fangs."

"I like peace," said Walter, and he smiled his two-perfectly-matched-fangs smile. "Nobody bites me, and I don't bite anybody."

"Walter is perfect,"
said his mother.

One day Wyatt the Fox, who lived in another forest, happened by. He saw Walter and his mother in front of their house. Walter was practicing his violin.

Wyatt looked closely at Walter. "Those are terrific fangs you have," he said. "You really should do something with them."

Walter went on practicing his violin.

"You really should exercise those teeth," said Wyatt.

"Everybody says that," said Walter, putting down his violin. "I eat a lot of crunchy foods when I can find them."

"But you need something you can really sink your teeth into," said Wyatt. "And I have an idea—for both of us. With my brains and your fangs, we can't lose."

"Wyatt the Fox, I don't trust you," said Walter's mother.

But Walter said, "Maybe it will be easier than being perfect, Mother."

"You can't be sure about that, Walter," she said.
"But maybe you should find out for yourself." She
started to go into the house. Then she turned and
said, "Wyatt the Fox, from the bottom of my heart,
I don't trust you."

After Walter's mother had left, Wyatt said to Walter, "You and I are going into business. And the business is biting. My boy, you are going to be a professional biter. And I am going to be your manager."

"But I like peace," said Walter.

"Do you want to spend the rest of your life being perfect?" asked Wyatt.

"Well, not exactly," said Walter.

Wyatt wrote a sign and hung it from the branch of a large tree. The sign read:

Walter looked at the sign. "I don't know how to bark," he said.

"Still, it makes a very impressive sign," said
Wyatt. "Now anyone who has an enemy and doesn't
want to go after him can come to you to do it. One
look at your fangs will convince them you can do
a good piece of work. And you'll be performing a
useful service, my boy."

"Yes," said Walter. "And everybody will say,
'Walter's fangs have a job.' "

When Walter's mother saw the sign she said, "Walter, you're making a terrible mistake. Biting is not for you. Playing the violin and biting don't mix."

"I have given up the violin," said Walter, "for biting."

"Just this very morning you were perfect," said Walter's mother, shaking her head. "Things change so fast in the forest."

Walter was sorry that his mother didn't approve. He hoped she would change her mind.

Walter sat under the tree with Wyatt, waiting
for business.

Soon Regina the Beaver came along. She looked at the sign. Then she looked at Walter's fangs. Then she said, "My neighbor, Naomi the Beaver, keeps taking my piles of wood. Can you help me?"

"Sure," said Walter. "First I'll ask her to give back the wood. Then if she doesn't, I'll bite her."

Regina looked at Walter's fangs again. "I believe in you," she said.

Walter rushed to Naomi's house. She was in her kitchen baking cakes.

"I've come to get back the piles of wood you took from Regina the Beaver," he said. "If you don't give them back, I'll bite you."

"If you bite me, I'll bite you back," said Naomi.
"You will?" said Walter.

"Yes," said Naomi. And she opened her mouth and showed two perfectly matched sharp front teeth.

"Don't you even want to run away from me?" asked Walter.

"No," said Naomi. *"You* go away. I'm busy."

"What about the wood?" asked Walter.

"That wood is mine," said Naomi. "It comes from my tree. Regina has her tree and I have my tree."

"She didn't tell me that," said Walter.

"Regina wants everyone's wood," said Naomi. "Well, don't just stand there with your tongue hanging out. As long as you're here, I'll give you some of my cake."

Walter sat down. "So you're in the bite business," said Naomi as she gave Walter a piece of cake. "I heard that you were a violin player."

"That was before I became a biter," said Walter. "Did you know that before I became a biter I was perfect?"

"I wouldn't want to be perfect. And I wouldn't want to be a biter," said Naomi. "Couldn't you think of something else to be?"

"What else is there?" asked Walter.

"Oh, there are lots of things to choose from," said Naomi, "if you use your head instead of your teeth."

"What do you know about anything," said
Walter, "hanging around a kitchen baking your
cakes."

"Baking is good, clean work," said Naomi.
"Biting isn't. It hurts!"

"So?" said Walter.

Suddenly she leaned toward Walter. "I'm doing this for your own good," she said. And she sunk her two perfectly matched sharp front teeth into Walter's tail.

"Owww! You bit me!" cried Walter. "Owww!" And he ran out of the house and into the forest.

"Eat and run, eat and run," sighed Naomi. And she swept up some cake crumbs from her kitchen floor.

Walter ran and ran. "Owww!" he cried.
"Owww!"

He ran into Wyatt. "What happened to you?"
asked Wyatt.

"I got bitten," said Walter.

"*You* got bitten?" said Wyatt. "Impossible.
Nobody bites Walter the Wolf."

"Well, then Naomi is nobody," said Walter.
"Owww!"

"Say, if she bites that well, maybe we could hire
her for our business," said Wyatt.

"Our business?" said
Walter. "There isn't any
business. I quit. Biting *hurts*."
    "But you could be the best
biter in the forest," said Wyatt.
"You can't quit."

"Well, maybe just one bite," said Walter. And
he sunk his fangs into Wyatt.

"Yeow!" cried Wyatt. "You're dangerous." And
he started to run, and he didn't stop until he was
out of the forest.

Just then Walter's mother came along. "What happened?" she asked.

"I'm not a biter any more, Mother," said Walter. "And I'm not perfect either."

"That's all right," said Walter's mother. "Nobody's perfect forever. You lasted a long time. Now let's go into the house and rest."

"In just a minute," said Walter.

He ran to the big tree where Wyatt the Fox had hung the sign. He reached up and pulled it down. He crossed out the words and wrote new ones. Then he hung the sign back up on the tree. The sign read:

WALTER the WOLF, ~~INC.~~

I HAVE BIG FANGS.
I DID NOT CHOOSE THEM,
BUT I CAN CHOOSE
NOT TO USE THEM.

Walter the Wolf

Then Walter went into his house and soaked his tail.